The Wizard
and the Flea
A Mexican Tale

First published in 2011
by Wayland

Text copyright © Jillian Powell
Illustration copyright © Elena Almazova
and Vitaly Shvarov

Wayland
338 Euston Road
London NW1 3BH

Wayland Australia
Level 17/207 Kent Street
Sydney, NSW 2000

Series Editor: Louise John
Editor: Katie Woolley
Cover design: Paul Cherrill
Design: D.R.ink
Consultant: Shirley Bickler

A CIP catalogue record for this book is available from the British Library.

ISBN 9780750265348

Printed in China

Wayland is a division of Hachette Children's Books,
an Hachette UK Company

www.hachette.co.uk

The Wizard and the Flea

A Mexican Tale

Written by Jillian Powell
Illustrated by Elena Almazova
and Vitaly Shvarov

WAYLAND

There once lived a wizard in a house high up on a hill. Everyone knew that the wizard was very clever indeed.

The wizard had a daughter and he loved her very much.

One day when she was out picking flowers, a young man called Rafa saw her.

At once, with just one look, he fell in love.

"She is the girl I will marry," he said to himself.

So, the next day, Rafa climbed
the steps to the wizard's house.

He climbed and climbed and yet
he never seemed to reach the top.

That was because the wizard was
making more steps!

The wizard knew what Rafa was going to ask. The wizard loved his daughter so much that he wanted her to stay with him.

At long last, Rafa reached the top
of the hill. He knocked on the door
and waited for the wizard to answer.

"Wizard, I will love your daughter forever if you will let me marry her," Rafa said.

The wizard took off his hat and
he thought hard.

"Not so fast," he said. "First you must show me that you can out-smart me. Only then can you marry my daughter."

"How can I do that?" Rafa asked.

"Tonight you must sleep in a place where I cannot find you!" the wizard said.

"Very well," Rafa smiled, for the wizard did not know that he had magic powers, too.

That night Rafa climbed into the cradle of the moon and rocked himself to sleep.

It didn't take long for the
wizard to find him.

The next night Rafa slept in a shell deep at the very bottom of the sea.

Still the wizard found him!

The third night Rafa turned himself into a flea.

The wizard was trying out a spell when the flea hopped into the brim of his hat and fell asleep.

All night the wizard looked for Rafa and cast spells to find him. But the wizard could not find him anywhere.

The night passed and when the sun rose, the flea hopped out of the wizard's hat and changed back into Rafa.

"Here I am," Rafa said. "I have slept beside you all night and you still couldn't find me."

The wizard was puzzled but
he had not found Rafa. He had
to let Rafa marry his daughter.

After they were married, they both
slept the first night in the cradle of
the moon.

The second night they slept in a shell at the bottom of the sea.

On the third night, two little fleas fell asleep in the brim of the wizard's hat.

They woke each day with the rising sun, and lived together happily for the rest of their lives.